What's the HuRRy, MuRRAy?

WHAT'S THE HURRY, MURRAY?

Text by Anna Prudente-Poulton

Additional text and concept design by Anna Martin

Illustrations by Josiane Vlitos

An Hachette UK Company
www.hachette.co.uk

Vie Books, an imprint of Summersdale Publishers Ltd
Part of Octopus Publishing Group Limited
Carmelite House
50 Victoria Embankment
LONDON
EC4Y 0DZ
UK

www.summersdale.com

Printed and bound in China

ISBN: 978-1-80007-016-5

Substantial discounts on bulk quantities of Summersdale books are available to corporations, professional associations and other organizations. For details contact general enquiries: telephone: +44 (0) 1243 771107 or email: enquiries@summersdale.com.

What's the HURRY, MURRAY?

A Child's Guide to Finding Calm

A My Healthy Mind Book

Anna Adams

vie

Josiane Vlitos

"What are you doing, Murray?" asked Hoots.

"My new friend Florrie is coming round and she LOVES butterflies, so I'm trying to catch some for her," said Murray.

"OK, but why are all your toys in the garden?" asked Hoots.

"I must tidy my playhouse before she arrives," Murray replied.

"OK, but Murray, **why** is there a **saucepan** by the **flower bed?**" asked Hoots.

Hoots only just got the question out before MURRAY SHOUTED...

5

"I'm so sorry for shouting at you, Hoots!" cried Murray.

"Murray, have you EATEN this morning?" asked Hoots.

"I can't EAT because my tummy is rolling around –
like a pea on a plate!" said Murray.

"Did you SLEEP well?"
asked Hoots.

"I didn't sleep at all!
My thoughts kept RUSHING
around and I couldn't get them
to slow down," Murray wept.

7

"The matter with you,"
said Hoots kindly,
"is that you have got yourself
in a huge tizzy."

"A huge what?"
sniffed Murray.

"A tizzy.
Tell me, does your head feel
FIZZY?"
asked Hoots.

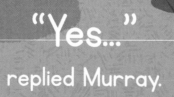

"Yes..."
replied Murray.

"Do you feel a little **DIZZY?**" asked Hoots.

"Yes..." answered Murray.

"Then you're in **a tizzy!**" Hoots said.

"But Hoots, I don't want to be in this **tizzy!** Can you please get me out of it?" said Murray.

9

"Of course I can!
Tell me what you're
worried about," said Hoots.

"Oh, Hoots, I really haven't got the time –
I need to..." Murray stopped,
as he rushed off with a saucepan.

"What's the hurry, Murray?
You're not getting ANYTHING
done because you're in
such a tizzy!" said Hoots.

"I can't get it out of my head. It's all such
A JUMBLE
that I don't know where to start!" cried Murray.

"OK," said Hoots, "When is your friend arriving?"

"This afternoon!" shouted Murray, "and I've got..."

"No," said Hoots, "DON'T RUSH, we have plenty of time."

Murray and Hoots sat on the bench together.

"Murray, can you tell me why you're in a **tizzy**?" asked Hoots, calmly.

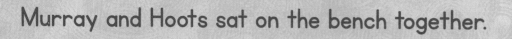

"It started when I was tidying my playhouse. Then I looked outside and realized that there weren't enough butterflies in the garden! I worried about running out of time to do everything, then I..." Murray stopped to take a breath.

"Oh Murray," said Hoots, "you're working yourself into a **tizzy** again."

"That's it," said Murray, "I begin one task, but then I worry about another and everything gets worse and worse."

13

"I can't do anything right and my friend will be bored and will never visit me again," sighed Murray.

"Florrie is lucky to have a friend as KIND as you," said Hoots.

"Don't be in such a hurry, Murray, and I promise you that **everything will be OK.**"

"Really, Hoots? But my friend is coming *this afternoon!*" said Murray.

"It's not **what** you have to do, it's HOW you do it that matters the most," said Hoots.

"We will write a list of what we need to do. Firstly though, we must help you **calm down** so that you can think clearly again."

"Shall we try some exercises to calm down, Murray?"
asked Hoots.

"Breathe in through
your nose until your
tummy is round –
like a balloon!"
said Hoots.

"As you breathe out
through your mouth,
imagine blowing the
balloon out of your
tummy, and watch it float
far away into the sky."

"Good!" said Hoots.
"Can you see your balloon
gliding away, Murray?"

"YES!" said Murray. "I'd like to make another one."

Murray breathed in slowly and then out again,
and watched his balloons fly away from him.

17

Hoots fetched Murray
some water and a nice
ripe apple from the tree.

"Before you get going again,
drink this water and eat this apple.
You will feel MUCH BETTER
after a **drink** and some
food," said Hoots.

Murray

18

"Mmm, I am beginning to feel **more like me**," said Murray.

"That's good!" replied Hoots.

"So, Murray," said Hoots, "try to IMAGINE what you want to happen when your friend arrives."

"I see her coming into the garden and us **playing** with my toys. Then I think we will admire all the **butterflies** flitting around us," said Murray.

"OK, so all you need to do is tidy the garden, get your toys ready and catch some butterflies," said Hoots. "That will all be **simple** if you do ONE THING AT A TIME!"

"I suppose so, but..." stuttered Murray.

"Murray, don't get yourself into a tizzy again," reminded Hoots.

"But Hoots!
What about the butterflies?
What if the toys I pick out
aren't ones she likes? Florrie is
here for a whole afternoon..."

"What's the hurry, Murray?"
asked Hoots. "If your friend is here for
a whole afternoon, then you can take
your time and enjoy all your toys."

"Maybe Florrie would like
to help catch butterflies
as well?" added Hoots.

"Oh! I hadn't thought of that," said Murray. Thank you, Hoots, I'm feeling SO MUCH BETTER now. My tummy has stopped rolling and **I'm not in a tizzy.**"

"Great! But please remember, Murray, that if you ever feel **overwhelmed** again, you should always ask for HELP," said Hoots.

"What does overwhelmed mean, Hoots?" asked Murray.

"It's when it feels like a **big wave** keeps crashing above you and **knocking you** off your feet over and over every time you try to **stand up**," said Hoots.

"Oh Hoots!" said Murray,
"that's what I was feeling,
that overwhelmed thing!"

"Yes, and I'll be here for you
if you feel it again," added Hoots.

25

"Hoots?"

"Yes, Murray?"

"Maybe I could ask Florrie how she gets butterflies into her garden and ask her to help me do the same here," said Murray.

"That's a **great idea**," agreed Hoots, "it's always much more fun to do things TOGETHER."

"Hoots?"

"Yes, Murray?"

"I think I might have **a nap** before
I tidy and get my toys ready for Florrie,"
yawned Murray.

"Another EXCELLENT idea,
Murray," said Hoots.

"I can help you this morning, Murray."

"Thank you, Hoots, I'm so lucky to have you as a friend," said Murray.

"Friends are there to **help**, but you need to **ask!**" exclaimed Hoots.

"Murray?"
said Hoots.

"Yes, Hoots?"
mumbled Murray.

"Would you like me to start tidying
the garden?" asked Hoots.

"ZZZZ ZZZZ ZZZZZZ ZZZZZZ."

"Oh, Murray, you **were tired!**" said Hoots,
"I'll ask this frog if he wouldn't mind waking
you up when Florrie is on her way."

Later that day...

Have you enjoyed reading this book with your child?
If so, why not write a review on your favourite website?

If you're interested in finding out more about our books,
find us on Facebook at **Summersdale Publishers**,
on Twitter at **@Summersdale** and
on Instagram at **@summersdalebooks**
and get in touch. We'd love to hear from you!

Thanks very much for buying this Summersdale book.
www.summersdale.com